For
Noah x

LITTLE TIGER PRESS
1 The Coda Centre, 189 Munster Road,
London SW6 6AW
www.littletiger.co.uk
First published in Great Britain 2001
This edition published 2013
Text and illustrations copyright ©
Tim Warnes 2001
Visit Tim Warnes at
www.ChapmanandWarnes.com
Tim Warnes has asserted his right
to be identified as the author
and illustrator of this work under the
Copyright, Designs and Patents Act, 1988
Printed in China • LTP/1800/0616/0513
ISBN 978-1-84895-735-0
2 4 6 8 10 9 7 5 3 1

Can't You Sleep, Dotty?

Tim Warnes

★ ★ ★

LITTLE TIGER PRESS
London

Dotty couldn't sleep.
It was her first night
in her new home.

Tick!

Tick!

She tried sleeping
upside down.

She tried
snuggling up
to Penguin.

She even tried
lying on the
floor.

AWOOOOOOOOOOOOO

But still Dotty
couldn't sleep.

Dotty's howling woke up Pip the mouse. "Can't you sleep, Dotty?" he asked. "Perhaps you should try counting the stars like I do."

But Dotty could
only count up to
one. *That* wasn't
enough to send
her to sleep.

What could she do next?

AWOOOOOOOOOOOO

Susie the bird was awake now.
"Can't you sleep, Dotty?" she twittered.
"I always have a little drink before
  I go to bed."

Chirp!

Chirp!

Dotty went to her bowl and
had a little drink.

Slurp!
Slurp!

But then she made a little puddle. Well *that* didn't help! What *could* Dotty do to get to sleep?

AWOOOOOOOOOOO

Whiskers the rabbit had woken
up, too. "Can't you sleep, Dotty?"
he mumbled sleepily. "I hide
away in my burrow at bedtime.
That always works."

Dotty dived under her blanket
so that only her bottom was
showing. But it was all
dark under there with
no light at all.

Boing!

Dotty was too scared to go to sleep.

AWOOOOOOOOOOOOOOOO

Flump!

Tommy the tortoise
poked his head
from out of
his shell.

"Can't you sleep, Dotty?" he sighed.
"I like to sleep where it's bright
and sunny."

Plod
Plod

Dotty liked that idea . . .

. . . and turned on her torch!

"Turn it off, Dotty!"
shouted all her friends.
"*We* can't get to sleep now!"

Poor Dotty was too
tired to try anything else.
Then Tommy had a great idea . . .

he helped Dotty into her bed.
What Dotty needed for the first
night in her new home was . . .

. . . to snuggle up among *all* her new friends.

Soon they were all fast asleep.

Night night, Dotty.

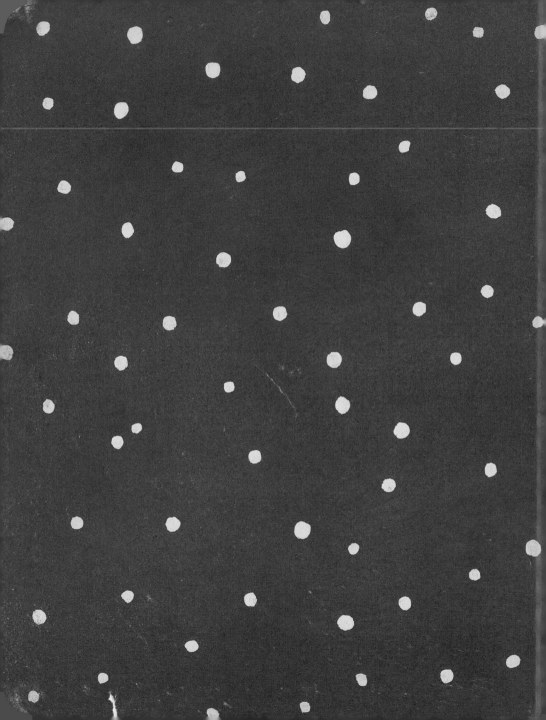